TSUBASA

CLAMP

TRANSLATED AND ADAPTED BY
Anthony Gerard

LETTERED BY
Dana Hayward

BALLANTINE BOOKS • NEW YORK

Tsubasa crosses over with *xxxHOLiC*. Although it isn't necessary to read *xxxHOLiC* to understand the events in *Tsubasa*, you'll get to see the same events from different perspectives if you read both!

A Del Rey® Book
Published by The Random House Publishing Group
Copyright © 2004 CLAMP. All rights reserved.

First published in Japan in 2003 by Kodansha Ltd., Tokyo.
This publication — rights arranged through Kodansha Ltd.

All rights reserved under International and Pan-American
Copyright Conventions. Published in the United States by Del Rey Books,
an imprint of The Random House Publishing Group, a division of Random
House, Inc., New York, and simultaneously in Canada by Random House
of Canada Limited, Toronto.

Del Rey is a registered trademark and the Del Rey colophon
is a trademark of Random House, Inc.

www.delreymanga.com

Library of Congress Control Number: 2004094894

ISBN 0-345-47182-2

Manufactured in the United States of America

9 8 7 6 5 4 3 2 1

First Edition: September 2004

Contents

Honorifics Explained   iv

Chapitre 6   3

Chapitre 7   23

Chapitre 8   55

Chapitre 9   75

Chapitre 10   95

Chapitre 11   115

Chapitre 12   147

Chapitre 13   169

About the Creators   188

Past Works   189

Translation Notes   190

Preview of *Tsubasa* Volume 3   195

Honorifics Explained

Throughout the Del Rey Manga books, you will find Japanese honorifics left intact in the translations. For those not familiar with how the Japanese use honorifics, and more important, how they differ from American honorifics, we present this brief overview.

Politeness has always been a critical facet of Japanese culture. Ever since the feudal era, when Japan was a highly stratified society, use of honorifics — which can be defined as polite speech that indicates relationship or status — has played an essential role in the Japanese language. When addressing someone in Japanese, an honorific usually takes the form of a suffix attached to one's name (example: "Asuna-san"), or as a title at the end of one's name or in place of the name itself (example: "Negi-sensei," or simply "Sensei!").

Honorifics can be expressions of respect or endearment. In the context of manga and anime, honorifics give insight into the nature of the relationship between characters. Many translations into English leave out these important honorifics, and therefore distort the "feel" of the original Japanese. Because Japanese honorifics contain nuances that English honorifics lack, it is our policy at Del Rey not to translate them. Here, instead, is a guide to some of the honorifics you may encounter in Del Rey Manga.

-san: This is the most common honorific, and is equivalent to Mr., Miss, Ms., Mrs., etc. It is the all-purpose honorific and can be used in any situation where politeness is required.

-sama: This is one level higher than "-san." It is used to confer great respect.

-dono: This comes from the word "tono," which means "lord." It is even a higher level than "-sama," and confers utmost respect.

-kun: This suffix is used at the end of boys' names to express familiarity or endearment. It is also sometimes used by men among friends, or when addressing someone younger or of a lower station.

-chan: This is used to express endearment, mostly toward girls. It is also used for little boys, pets, and even among lovers. It gives a sense of childish cuteness.

Bozu: This is an informal way to refer to a boy, similar to the English term "kid" or "squirt."

Sempai: This title suggests that the addressee is one's "senior" in a group or organization. It is most often used in a school setting, where underclassmen refer to their upperclassmen as "sempai." It can also be used in the workplace, such as when a newer employee addresses an employee who has seniority in the company.

Kohai: This is the opposite of "-sempai," and is used toward underclassmen in school or newcomers in the workplace. It connotes that the addressee is of lower station.

Sensei: Literally meaning "one who has come before," this title is used for teachers, doctors, or masters of any profession or art.

-[blank]: Usually forgotten in these lists, but perhaps the most significant difference between Japanese and English. The lack of honorific means that the speaker has permission to address the person in a very intimate way. Usually, only family, spouses, or very close friends have this kind of permission. Known as *yobisute*, it can be gratifying when someone who has earned the intimacy starts to call one by one's name without an honorific. But when that intimacy hasn't been earned, it can also be very insulting.

RESERVoir CHRoNiCLE

Chapitre.6
Strength of the Heart

I'M SHÔGO ASAGI.

YOU?

...... SYAORAN.

SSSHHHH

I LIKE YOUR STYLE.

SSSHHHHHH

AND IT WAS JUST GETTING GOOD.

SIGH

SHÔGO, THE COPS!

HOOOSH

NEXT TIME WE'LL MEET, WE'LL HAVE SOME REAL FUN!

HOLD IT!!

TMP TMP TMP

TMP

TUMP

COME ON, YA BASTARDS! LET'S GET OUTTA HERE!

FOWOOO!!

GHOOOOO

FWOOM

SHULOOM

IT...
WENT...
INSIDE
ME.

I'M NOT
SURE. BUT I
SUDDENLY
GOT VERY
HOT...

THAT'S A
"KUDAN,"
HUH?

THAT WAS
AMAZING!
SYAORAN-
KUN, DID
THAT COME
FROM YOU?

IT PROBABLY GOT STEPPED ON SOMEWHERE AROUND HERE.

LIKE SOME DISCARDED PORK BUN.

AAAH!

WHAT A PAIN!

SKRITCH SKRITCH

NOOOO

LOOK.

THE TRUTH IS QUITE DIFFERENT.

NOW, WHERE CAN MY "ALMOST KUDAN" HAVE GOTTEN OFF TO?

HMM?

GLANCE

GASP

MOKONA!!

KYAA!

KYAA!

KYAA!

IT'S SO CUTE!

THE SWEET- EST THING!

LOOK HOW SOFT!

MOKONA IS POPULAR WITH THE LADIES!

しょんぼり

GLOOM

OH...
I SEE.

DID YOU
FIGURE
OUT WHO
HAD IT?

IT
WAS
...

BUT
MOKONA
DOESN'T
FEEL IT
ANYMORE.

ブ
ブ
ブ

SHAKE SHAKE
SHAKE

DON'T
KNOW.

YES!

MOKONA
WILL GO
ALL-OUT!

AND IF
YOU SENSE
ANYTHING
MORE, LET
US KNOW.

THUMP

STILL,
WE NOW
KNOW THAT
SOMEONE
CLOSE BY
HAS IT.

HMM.

EVEN IF WE
LIMIT IT TO THE
PEOPLE WHO
WERE HERE, IT'LL
STILL BE A
LONG SEARCH.

THERE
WERE LOTS
OF PEOPLE.

THAT'S
PRETTY
GOOD
PROG-
RESS.

え？！

EHP!

OKONO-MIYAKI IS A STAPLE OF THE DIET IN THE HANSHIN REPUBLIC.

IF YOU DON'T KNOW, THEN THAT MUST MEAN...

あのあの

UMM... UMM...

I ORDERED MODAN-YAKI, BUT MAYBE TONPEI-YAKI WOULD HAVE BEEN BETTER.

Y'SEE... OKONOMIYAKI IS *MY* FAVORITE DISH, SO...

"OKONO-MIYAKI"?

IS THAT WHAT THIS IS CALLED?

SSSZZZ

WHAT IS...

STARE

B-BMP

B-BMP

THEY PATROL THEIR TERRITORY MAKING SURE NO BAD KIDS CAUSE TROUBLE.

AND IF BAD PEOPLE ARE AROUND, THEY TAKE CARE OF THE PROBLEM!

THERE...

...THERE ARE BAD TEAMS, BUT THERE ARE GOOD TEAMS, TOO!

BUT THINK OF THE LIVES PUT IN DANGER WHEN THEY FIGHT IN SUCH A LARGE PUBLIC PLACE.

THAT'S BECAUSE I'M JUST USELESS.

♪ THIS OKONOMIYAKI LOOKS GREAT!

LIKE A LOCAL MILITIA?

WHAT ABOUT THOSE TWO TEAMS BEFORE?

THAT'S TRUE, HUH?

MASAYOSHI-KUN HERE WAS IN BIG TROUBLE.

WHEN THEY BATTLE OTHER TEAMS, SOME OF THE SURROUNDING BUILDINGS GET DAMAGED, SO THE ADULTS ARE AFRAID OF THEM... BUT THEY WOULDN'T DO ANYTHING ELSE THAT'S BAD!

THEY'RE REALLY COOL!

BUT THE ONES IN GOGGLES AREN'T LIKE THEM AT ALL!

THE ONES IN CAPS WERE THE BAD ONES!

OH!

SMELLS GREAT!

STARE

IT'S SO BIG AND STRONG... EVERYONE WISHES THEY HAD A KUDAN JUST LIKE IT!

ESPECIALLY THEIR LEADER, SHÔGO-SAN! THEY SAY HIS KUDAN IS SPECIAL LEVEL!

I-I SURE DO!

LOOK AT ALL THE CABBAGE!

STAAAARE

I... I'M SORRY.

ZLIP ZLIP

SLUMP

STARE

BLUSH

THUMPA

THUMPA THUMPA

STARE

AND YOU WISH YOU HAD A FRIEND JUST LIKE HIM, HUH?

EH?

BUT I'D ALSO LIKE A FRIEND LIKE SYAORAN-KUN!

...IS JUST AMAZING!

ANYBODY WITH A SPECIAL LEVEL KUDAN...

SO, WHAT IS THAT? SPECIAL LEVEL?

HMM.

DIDN'T THE LEADER OF THAT GOGGLE TEAM SAY SOMETHING ABOUT A SPECIAL KUDAN...?

STARE

IT'S AN ESPECIALLY HIGH LEVEL FOR KUDAN.

特級

一級

二級

三級

四級

...AND AT THE VERY TOP IS THE SPECIAL LEVEL.

AND MOVING UP, THERE'S THE THIRD LEVEL, SECOND LEVEL, FIRST LEVEL...

THE FOURTH-LEVEL KUDAN IS THE LOWEST.

THEN...

...THAT LEADER'S KUDAN MUST BE VERY STRONG.

YEARS AGO, ALL THE COUNTRIES GOT TOGETHER AND BANNED THE USE OF LEVELS ON KUDAN...

...BUT NORMAL PEOPLE STILL USE THE SYSTEM.

TWITCH

YEAH!

19

NOW THAT YOU MEN- TION IT...

BUT *WHEN* DID SYAORAN- KUN'S KUDAN JOIN UP WITH HIM?

I HAD AN ODD DREAM LAST NIGHT.

A DREAM?

STOP RIGHT THERE !!

Chapitre.7
Linked Worlds

RESERVoir CHRoNiCLE

AND THE GUY WITH HIM WAS THE HIGH PRIEST...

IS THAT RIGHT...?

WITH OKONOMIYAKI HERE, THE WAITERS DO ALL THE COOKING FOR YOU.

YOU DON'T HAVE TO DO ANYTHING.

BUSTLE

"YOUR MAJESTY"! THAT SOUNDS COOL!

LEAVE IT, WILL YAP

YES...

MAJESTY... WAS HE A KING IN YOUR WORLD?

IT'S JUST LIKE THE SPACE-TIME WITCH SAID...

SHADDUP!

YOU GOT YELLED AT!

"...THEY'VE DEVELOPED UNDER COMPLETELY DIF- FERENT CONDITIONS ON OTHER WORLDS."

"PEOPLE YOU'VE MET ON YOUR WORLD..."

THE TWO FROM SYAORAN'S WORLD LIVED A COMPLETELY DIFFERENT LIFE THAN THESE TWO.

EXCUSE ME? ? - ?

THEY'RE THE SAME... AND NOT THE SAME.

YOU'RE SAYING THAT THEY'RE THE SAME AS THE KING AND HIGH PRIEST OF THE KID'S WORLD?

...AT THE VERY BASIC LEVEL, THEY'RE THE SAME.

I GUESS.

BUT WHEN IT COMES DOWN TO IT...

"SOUL"!

THAT'S WHAT YOU'RE SAYING, RIGHT?

THEIR NATURE... THEIR HEARTS...

THE VERY ROOT OF THEIR LIVES.

BASIC LEVEL?

DON'T YOU DARE!

FROM NOW ON, I'M CALLING YOU, "YOUR MAJESTY."

I WONDER IF HIS MAJESTY AND THE HIGH PRIEST ARE ALL RIGHT.

YES.

THOSE TWO WOULD MAKE SURE EVERYTHING'S FINE.

DID THE COUNTRY CARRY ON ALL RIGHT AFTER THE FIGHT?

ARE YOU GUYS GOING SOMEWHERE?

YES.

I THOUGHT WE WOULD SEARCH IN THIS SECTION OF TOWN.

NOW...

WHAT'S THE PLAN FROM HERE?

WE DON'T REALLY KNOW. WE'RE SEARCHING FOR SOMETHING.

WHERE WOULD THAT BE?

UH... EXCUSE ME.

BUT WE DON'T KNOW OUR WAY AROUND, SO WE WON'T BE ABLE TO GO FAR.

HM.

WE HAVE TO BE ABLE TO FIND OUR WAY BACK TO SORA CHAN'S APARTMENT.

BUT I SHOULD PHONE HOME FIRST.

IF YOU'D JUST WAIT HERE A SECOND...

WE DON'T WANT TO PUT YOU OUT...

NOT AT ALL!

IF IT'S OKAY WITH YOU, I'LL HELP YOU LOOK.

I CAN SHOW YOU AROUND.

TMP

HE REALLY *DOES* WANT TO BE FRIENDS, HUH?

HELLO? HELLO? HELLO?

MOKONA WILL MAKE A PHONE CALL, TOO!

TMP TMP TMP

STARE

IT WAS ABOUT THAT CREATURE THAT APPEARED...

...THAT BEAST OF FIRE.

I NEARLY FORGOT.

OUR CONVER-SATION WAS CUT OFF.

YOU WERE TALKING ABOUT YOUR DREAM...

YES...

STAMP

ME, AS WELL.

IT WAS VERY PERSISTENT.

I WANNA KNOW WHO THIS "SYAORAN" IS.

IF YOU'RE TALKING ABOUT DREAMS OF WEIRD ANIMALS... I HAD ONE, TOO.

YOU HAVE BUSINESS WITH HIM?

ARE YOU THE ONE WHO SHÔGO SAID HE "LIKES YOUR STYLE"?

DOOM

······

HEH HEH HENH

AND WHAT IF I AM?

DOOM

I'LL TAKE YOU ON!

BUT...

...KUROGANE-SAN!

YOU GAVE YOUR SWORD TO THAT WOMAN...

SHUT UP, OVER THERE!

ZAPH

THE HANSHIN REPUBLIC IS JUST HIS STYLE, HUH?

KUROGANE'S BEEN LOOKING FORWARD TO THIS!

HE WASN'T BORED AT ALL!

IT'S A TEAM THAT WANTS TO CONTROL THIS DISTRICT!

THEY'RE BATTLING SHŌGO'S TEAM OVER IT!

MASAYOSHI-KUN, DO YOU KNOW THIS GUY?

SYAORAN-KUN!!

IS THEIR LEADER ANY GOOD?

YAAAHH

YAAAHH

YAAAHH

TAKE A LOOK AT THE ATTACK OF A FIRST-LEVEL KUDAN!

EAT THIS!!

HE MAY NOT LOOK LIKE MUCH, BUT HIS KUDAN IS ONE OF THE FASTEST AROUND!

AND...

HIS KUDAN IS *FIRST LEVEL!*

43

KANI DÔRAKU!!*

JAA KIIIIN

*CRAB FREE-STYLE

KUROGANE SAN!!

WHERE'S *YOUR* KUDAN?

YOU'RE PROBABLY SO WEAK, YOU'RE ASHAMED TO BRING IT OUT!

AHHHHH HA HA

HA HA HA

KRMBLE

KRMBLE

HAMA
RYÛ-
Ô-JIN
!!*

*MAGIC WAVE: DRAGON KING SWORD

GAAAAAAAAAAAA!!

Chapitre.8
The Country Where Gods Live

WE'RE
BACK!

KACHAK

YES!

WERE
YOU ABLE
TO FIND
ANY CLUES?

TMP TMP
TMP

WE'RE
BACK!

WE'RE
BACK!

SST

WELCOME.
COME
ON IN.

OH!
YOU'RE
ALL HERE!

HOW'D
IT GO?

...BEFORE ANY OF THAT...

BUT...

MMMMM!

WHERE'S MY "WELCOME HOME" KISS?!

HONEY!!

PUT IT HERE, BABE!

YOU *HAD* A REACTION, BUT IT DISAPPEARED.

I SEE...

THAT BEAST MUST HAVE BEEN YOUR KUDAN, SYAORAN-KUN.

THAT'S RIGHT.

WHAT A HUGE BUMP! ARASHI'S REALLY STRONG

AND...

...JUST WHEN SYAORAN WAS IN TROUBLE, SOMETHING THAT LOOKED LIKE A BEAST OF FIRE SUDDENLY APPEARED.

AND KUROGANE'S KUDAN ALSO SEEMS STRONG!

IT SEEMS LIKE A PRETTY STRONG ONE, TOO!

WELL...

HOW DO YOU KNOW THAT?

IT'S MY BELIEF...

...THAT KUDAN ARE AKIN TO GODS IN THIS NATION.

I TOLD YOU BEFORE...

...I'M A SCHOLAR OF HISTORY.

THE KUDAN ARE THE LINCHPIN OF THE WHOLE THING.

IN THE HANSHIN REPUBLIC, THERE IS A MYTH THAT'S BEEN HANDED DOWN THROUGH THE AGES...

IT SAYS THAT THE NUMBER OF KAMI, GODS, IS "YAOYOROZU."

"YAOYOROZU"?

八百万

IT'S SPELLED WITH THE CHARACTERS FOR "EIGHT MILLION."

THEY SAY THERE ARE AS MANY GODS AS THERE ARE THINGS AND PHENOMENA IN THE WORLD.

NO, PROBABLY MANY MORE.

...KAMI-SAMA!

LOTS OF...

SO THERE ARE EIGHT MILLION GODS HERE?

THE WORD "YAOYOROZU" REALLY SIMPLY MEANS, "A WHOLE LOT."

THAT'S PRETTY IMPRESSIVE.

YOU LIVE TOGETHER WITH YOUR GODS.

SO THE GODS OF THAT MYTH ARE NOW CALLED KUDAN?

SO THE GODS OF THIS LAND...

...PROTECT EACH AND EVERY PERSON WHO LIVES IN IT!

WHOOSH

YOU CAME TO THAT CONCLUSION, TOO?

THE KUDAN, OR RATHER THE GODS, HAVE A LASTING LOVE FOR THE PEOPLE OF THIS COUNTRY!

I'VE THOUGHT THAT ALL ALONG!

.....

YES.

EVERY PERSON, WITHOUT EXCEPTION, IS ACCOMPANIED BY A KUDAN.

SO EVERY HUMAN IN THIS COUNTRY IS PROTECTED!

NOT ONE IS LEFT ALONE!

THEY HATE LOSING; THEY NEVER GET TO THE POINT; THEY'LL ATTACK IF YOU'RE NOT PAYING ATTENTION; IF OUR TEAM WINS THEY GO CRAZY; THEY THROW THEMSELVES IN THE RIVER...

IT'S TRUE...

...THAT A LOT OF PEOPLE IN THE HANSHIN REPUBLIC ARE EASY TO GET RILED UP.

BUT EVEN SO...

...I THINK THEY REALLY ARE GOOD PEOPLE.

AND THAT'S WHY...

...WHEN IT COMES TO FINDING SAKURA'S FEATHER...

...SEARCHING HERE IS PROBABLY BETTER THAN SEARCHING IN A COUNTRY FULL OF BAD PEOPLE, OR A COUNTRY THAT MAKES WAR ON ITS NEIGHBORS.

GASP

A KUDAN!

IS THAT WHAT YOU MEAN?

AND IF A KUDAN DISAPPEARED, THE WAVE MIGHT DISAPPEAR, TOO.

MAKES SENSE.

なるほど...

A KUDAN *CAN* APPEAR AND DISAPPEAR.

BUT WE HAVE NO IDEA JUST WHO HAD THE KUDAN WITH THE FEATHER.

IT WAS IN THE MIDDLE OF A TERRITORIAL BATTLE.

THERE WERE WHOLE LOTS OF KUDAN BACK THERE!

...WE MAY FIND SAKURA'S FEATHER!

WITHIN ONE OF THESE KUDAN...

63

TODAY WE HAVE BEEF UDON NOODLES AND FRIED TOFU SUSHI.

I MADE ALL THE ARRANGEMENTS BEFORE GOING OFF TO WORK.

I WILL NEED THE HELP OF KUROGANE AND FAI.

ALL RIGHT!

SINCE WE'VE GOT THAT ALL DECIDED, IT'S TIME TO FORTIFY OURSELVES WITH SOME GOOD FOOD!

FSSH

YOU WERE AWAY FROM SAKURA ALL DAY.

YOU WERE WORRIED, WEREN'T YOU?

NOT TODAY, YOU DON'T.

MOKONA'S GOING TO EAT, SO MOKONA WILL WORK!

IF YOU DON'T WORK, YOU DON'T EAT.

WHY DO I HAVE TO HELP?

I'LL HELP TOO.

WHEN DINNER IS READY, I'LL GIVE YOU A CALL.

YOU CAN STAY AND WATCH HER.

KREEE

THANKS! THANKS A LOT!

KACHAK

WERE YOU ABLE TO FIND WHAT YOU WERE LOOKING FOR AFTER I LEFT?

SYAORAN-KUN!!

MASA-YOSHI-KUN.

HUFF
WHEEZE
HUFF
WHEEZE
WHOOSH

NOT YET...

THAT'S PRETTY AMAZING!

MY KUDAN CAN FIND ANYBODY AS LONG AS HE'S MET THEM ONCE.

AMAZING!
AMAZING!

BUT THAT'S ABOUT *ALL* HE CAN DO.

HE'S PRETTY WEAK!

I'M SURPRISED YOU WERE ABLE TO FIND US.

IT'S NO GOOD IF IT'S TOO FAR AWAY, THOUGH.

ARE YOU SURE IT'S OKAY?

OKAY, THEN HOW ABOUT I BE YOUR GUIDE AGAIN TODAY?

SURE!

TODAY'S SUNDAY!

IT'S PERFECTLY FINE FOR TODAY!

BOING

71

Chapitre.9
The Magician's Kudan

BUT FOR SOME REASON, I DON'T UNDER- STAND THE WORDS!

NO, IT'S NOT THAT MY EARS HAVE GONE STRANGE.

AND IT'S NOT AS IF WE WENT ANYWHERE!

ABSOLUTELY CERTAIN, MA'AM!

HE WAS WITH THE SPIKY-HAIRED BIG GUY AND THE THIN BLOND GUY.

UMM...ARE YOU *SURE* THIS KID IS THE ONE?

THIS IS THE GUY SHÔGO SAID HE LIKED?

AND...

HMMMM.

WE HAVE A WINNER!

...THE SMALLEST ONE IN THE GROUP IS "SYAORAN."

SKRICH SKRICH

面倒◎▲！

ЖЪФЛ

I *KNEW* THEY WOULDN'T UNDER-STAND ME!

HANSHIN MAP

SUBWAY
HANSHIN CASTLE FRONT ENTRANCE STATION

HANSHIN CASTLE IS THIS WAY!

HANS
CAST

TMP TMP TMP TMP

WHOOM

ENTRANCE TO HANSHIN CASTLE

MOKONA!

MASAYOSHI-KUN!

BULUUUUN

YOU LOOK LIKE YOU'RE HAVING *FUN!*

AT LEAST THE WHITE THING DOES!

HEEEEY!

HOW'D YOU GET UP THERE!?

SO IT *IS* MOKONA THAT'S DOING IT.

I GET IT NOW.

AT LEAST WHAT YOU TWO ARE SAYING.

YEAH.

SO YOU UNDER-STAND ME NOW?

MOKONA IS PRETTY INCREDIBLE!

TRANSPORTING US TO OTHER WORLDS...

TRANSLATING OUR LANGUAGES FOR US...

EATING APPLES WHOLE...

SWING, SWING, I'M JUST LIKE A BALLOON!

AND BLOW SOME MORE!

BLOW, WIND, BLOW!

MOKONA WAS SERVING AS A TRANSLATION DEVICE.

THAT'S WHAT IT MEANS.

HEY!

DOES THIS MEAN THAT ANY TIME WE GET SEPARATED FROM IT, WE WON'T BE ABLE TO COMMUNICATE?

WHAT A PAIN!!

AWW!

TMP

86

Chapitre.10
Where the Feather Went

SWIP

EH?

LOOK UP THERE.

THAT WAS A SURPRISE.

A KUDAN CAN DO THAT?

THIS COUNTRY IS PRETTY AMAZING.

YOU LIKED THAT ATTACK, DIDN'T YOU, MOKONA?

PRIMELA-CHAN'S KUDAN IS SPECIAL LEVEL!

BE CAREFUL!

AMAZING!

AMAZING!

BBB BOOM

LOOK AT THAT DAMN GRIN!

THAT MAN IS A COMBAT VETERAN.

YEAAAH!

EH

THAT DOESN'T SURPRISE YOU?

BBOOM

I IMAGINE SO.

YEAAAH!

...THE LOOK IN HIS EYES JUST GIVES YOU THAT IMPRESSION.

THERE'S A CLUE IN THE CASUAL WAY FAI-SAN CARRIES HIMSELF...

...AND...

FAI-
SAN!!

KAKK

BBOOOM

FAI-
SAN!!

HISHS

HISHS

I'M ALL
RIGHT!

SHAKK

AND SINCE THIS GIRL IS FIGHTING WITH HER KUDAN, AND MOKONA ISN'T REACTING...

...IT MUST MEAN THAT THE GIRL ISN'T THE ONE WITH THE FEATHER.

I NEVER EXPECTED IT TO CHANGE FORM!

AND THOSE LETTERS SURE COME AFTER YOU!

WHIRL, WHIRL.

TWIRL, TWIRL. I'M JUST LIKE A WATER BALLOON!

IF I DID, WHAT WOULD HAPPEN NEXT?

DO YOU SURRENDER?

WELL?

AH HA HA!

SYAORAN-KUN HAS SOME IMPORTANT BUSINESS TO SEE THROUGH.

WE CAN'T HAVE THAT.

THEN I MOVE ON TO THE NEXT ONE TO DEFEAT, THIS "SYAORAN" GUY!

PRIMELA-CHAN!

PRIMELA-CHAN!

YEAH!

YEAH!

YEAH!

I'D REALLY RATHER THAT IT ENDS WITH ME.

...THEN I...

IF SO...

HEH

SWISH

THUMP

GWOOO

WILL JUST HAVE TO WIIIIIIIIN!!

Chapitre.11
The Kudan of Fire

RESERVoir CHRoNiCLE

117

WHAT WAS THAT?!

HUH? あー？

WHAT ARE THESE TWO SQUABBLING ABOUT?

WAFT

UHP UHP

YOU BREAK BUILDINGS ALL THE TIME, SHÔGO-KUN! DON'T TALK TO *ME* ALL HIGH AND MIGHTY!

SNFFL SNFFL SNFFL SNFFL SNFFL

L O V E

PRIMELA-CHAN

PRIMELA-CHAN'S IN LOVE WITH THAT TEAM LEADER, THERE!

...SINCE HE NEVER COMES TO SEE HER, SHE'S LONELY!!

BUT...

WARRAAH!

HM?

WHAT ARE YOU ALL CRYING OVER?

WAAAAH!

118

SO PROBABLY, THE TIME THAT IT PUTS OUT ITS GREATEST STRENGTH IS WHEN IT'S PROTECTING ITS OWNER.

SORATA-SAN SAID THAT KUDAN PROTECT THEIR OWNERS.

WHY ISN'T IT ONE FIXED STRENGTH?

BUT...

...IT GETS STRONGER AND THEN GETS WEAKER.

WHAT IS THAT SUPPOSED TO MEAN?

SO SOME KUDAN HAS TAKEN IT INSIDE ITSELF.

AND THAT MEANS...

...THE WAY TO FIND THE FEATHER IS THROUGH BATTLE!

FOWOOO!!

YOU GUYS, STAY OUTTA THIS, GOT ME?

READY!

POWER TO PROTECT SAKURA.

LIKE I SAID IN MY DREAM, I WANT POWER.

YOU'LL FIGHT ALONG-SIDE ME?

THAT WAS THE FIRST TIME I WAS EVER HIT LIKE THAT!

OH, MAN!

FWA

SOOM

TUMP

I'M FINE! I *TOLD* YOU TO STOP SCREAMING MY NAME!

YOU'LL RUIN YOUR VOICE JUST BEFORE A CONCERT!

SHÔGO-KUN!!

SHE'S SO CUTE!

DON'T TALK SO BIG! YOU'RE BREAKING STUFF TOO!

WHSSH

WH— WHO EVER SAID I *CARED* WHAT HAPPENS TO YOU?!

CUTE

WHSSH

CHATTER

CHATTER

141

WATCH OUT!!

GAGARASSH

RMMBL
RMMBL

KYAAAAAH!!

NO!

NOT WHEN THERE ARE PEOPLE TO PROTECT!!

I CAN'T LEAVE JUST TO SAVE MYSELF!

143

Chapitre 12

The Proof of Bravery

DID I HEAR RIGHT?

THE FEATHER'S IN THAT KUDAN?

IN *THAT* KUDAN?!

RMMMM

I THINK I SEE... EVEN WHEN HE USED HIS KUDAN TO FIND US, MOKONA DIDN'T DETECT IT.

BUT WHEN IT PROTECTS ITS MASTER...

THE TIME WHEN IT NEEDS THE MOST POWER IS WHEN IT IS PROTECTING SOMEONE IT CARES ABOUT FROM A LIFE-OR-DEATH SITUATION.

148

EVEN NOW, IT'S TRYING TO PROTECT HIM FROM THE CRUMBLING CASTLE.

YOU JUST PUT THAT BOY DOWN RIGHT NOW!

THE LAST TIME MOKONA DETECTED IT...

...WAS ALSO WHEN MASAYOSHI WAS IN A DANGEROUS SITUATION.

SAKURA'S FEATHER...

...IS INSIDE THAT!

GO BACK TO *NORMAL* ALREADY!

H-HEY, I'M ALL RIGHT!

I'M JUST *FINE!*

THE FEATHER HAD TOO MUCH POWER FOR IT.

THAT'S MORE KUDAN THAN MASA-YOSHI CAN CONTROL.

WHAT'S WRONG WITH THAT KUDAN?

WHAT'LL YOU DO NOW?

STOP IT!!

ONE SLIP UP AND YOU'RE DEAD!

HOW DO YOU INTEND TO FIGHT SOMETHING THAT BIG?

I WON'T DIE.

I'M GOING TO GET SAKURA'S FEATHER BACK.

I STILL HAVE SOMETHING TO SEE THROUGH.

I CAN'T DIE YET.

WHOOSH

SYAORAN-KUN HAS STRENGTH.

IN A LOT OF DIFFERENT WAYS.

...WHY THAT FIRE KUDAN CAME TO HIM.

DOOOM

I GET THE FEELING THAT I UNDERSTAND...

GLTTR

GLTTR

GWOOOO

IT'S SPARKLING.

STOP!!

I TOLD YOU TO STOP!!

WOBBL

DOOM

D-DOOM

SYAORAN-KUN!!

TMP

GASP

156

SYAORAN-
KUN!

FWRAA

SYAORAN-
KUN!

H-HOT!!

AH!

T— TAKE IT!!

GHOOOOH

...THEN I WANT YOU TO HAVE IT!

IF THE THING INSIDE MY KUDAN IS THE THING YOU'RE LOOKING FOR...

MASAYOSHI-KUN!

SO IF IT BURNS ME, LET IT BURN!!

162

SHÔGO'S KUDAN!

166

SHHHHHHHHH

THE *LEAST*
I COULD DO
WAS KEEP THE
PLACE FROM
CATCHING FIRE.

Chapitre.13
The Reason for Tears

170

AND AT THE MOMENT, YOU'VE LOST YOUR MEMORY. IT'S IN ORDER TO FIND YOUR MEMORIES THAT YOU'RE TRAVELING BETWEEN WORLDS.

ANOTHER... WORLD?

YOU ARE A PRINCESS FROM ANOTHER WORLD.

IF YOU'D BE SO KIND AS TO LISTEN, I'LL EXPLAIN.

YOU HAVE TRAVELING COMPANIONS.

NO...

BY MYSELF?

YES.

ARE YOU... ONE OF THOSE?

NICE TA MEETCHA!

SHAKE!

I'M KURO-GANE.

AND MAY I PRESENT—

MOKONA MODOKI! BUT YOU CAN SAY MOKONA!

SHUPP

AND THIS CUTE, FLUFFY ONE IS...

IT SEEMS ONE OF THE FEATHERS HAS BEEN RETURNED TO HER.

YES.

BUT IN THE PATHS TO COME, THERE IS NO GUARANTEE THAT THEY WILL BE AS LUCKY AS THEY WERE THIS TIME.

About the Creators

CLAMP is a group of four women who have become the most popular manga artists in America—Satsuki Igarashi, Mick Nekoi, Mokona Apapa, and Nanase Ohkawa. They started out as doujinshi (fan comics) creators, but their skill and craft brought them to the attention of publishers very quickly. Their first work from a major publisher was *RG Veda*, but their first mass success was with *Magic Knight Rayearth*. From there, they went on to write many series, including *Cardcaptor Sakura* and *Chobits*, two of the most popular manga in the United States. Like many Japanese manga artists, they prefer to avoid the spotlight, and little is known about them personally.

CLAMP is currently publishing three series in Japan: *Tsubasa* and *xxxHOLiC* with Kodansha and *Gohou Drug* with Kadokawa.

Past Works

CLAMP have created many series. Here is a brief overview of one of them.

X/1999

Kamui Shirou left Tokyo after the death of the mother of his friends, Fuma and Kotori. Now, six years later, Kamui is confronted by a vision of his own mother's death. Burning, she commands him to seek his destiny in Tokyo, and so he returns.

A turning point for the planet Earth is coming in the year 1999. Ravaged by mankind's carelessness, the planet is polluted and near death. The priestess Hinoto has seen two possible visions for humanity: In one, mankind is saved, and in the other, mankind is destroyed so that the earth can be born anew. The Seven Seals, or Dragons of Heaven, are pledged to fight for the preservation of humanity. The Seven Minions, or Dragons of Earth, want to exterminate all human life to make way for a new age.

Hinoto's vision centers on Kamui, who has the power to choose the world's fate. Pledged to protect his childhood friends Fuma and Kotori, Kamui finds allies in the form of Arashi and Sorata, two of the Seven Seals. (You've already met the Hanshin-reality versions of Arashi and Sorata (Sora) in *Tsubasa* volume 1.) For the sake of his friends, Kamui chooses to fight for the Seven Seals. Sadly, Fuma is Kamui's "twin star," his opposite number, and because Kamui chose the side of good for himself, Fuma is forced to join the side of evil, the Seven Minions. Thus Kamui must fight the friend he sought to save.

Acknowledged as one of CLAMP's most visually stunning manga, *X/1999* is set in the same world as *CLAMP School Detectives* and *Tokyo Babylon*, and is still an ongoing series. The manga has been adapted as an anime film and a TV series.

Translation Notes

Japanese is a tricky language for most Westerners, and translation is often more art than science. For your edification and reading pleasure, here are notes on some of the places where we could have gone in a different direction in our translation of the work, or where a Japanese cultural reference is used.

Kyaa!

"Kyaaaa" is standard onomatopoeia (sound word) for a scream in manga, but many Japanese people have adopted this sound and use it to express joy, surprise, and other happy emotions.

Tsuruhashi

The town in which our heroes stop by to eat okonomiyaki (see next entry) is called Tsuruhashi. In our world, Tsuruhashi is only about a kilometer south of Osaka Castle, and it is the station which connects the Osaka Loop Line that circles the city with the Kintetsu-Nara line which goes out to the suburbs between Osaka and Nara. Millions of people pass through this station, and because of that, it's only natural that the restaurants there are both famous and good!

Okonomiyaki

They call it Japanese pancakes or Japanese pizza, but the only thing similar between those and okonomiyaki is that all are round and flat. Okonomiyaki is made of flour, water, cabbage (mixed with other veggies), egg, seasonings, some kind of meat (seafood is common), and a delicious steak-sauce-like okonomiyaki sauce. The "konomi" means "like" or "love," and it indicates that you can put the veggies or meat you most like in it. The "yaki" means fried (the same as with "teriyaki" or "sukiyaki").

Flipping Rights

Most okonomiyaki that you will find in Japan is made in the kitchen, or at least, behind the counter. However, there are okonomiyaki restaurants where you can flip the okonomiyaki yourself. But since the dish was created in the Kansai (Osaka, Kyoto, Nara, Kobe) region, chefs jealously guard the right to flip their okonomiyaki—only when it's ready. After all, they are proud of their food and want it to be perfectly cooked.

Attack Names

Most anime, manga, and game fans are familiar with the attack names that the opponents shout at each other when making their attacks. Sure, it doesn't happen in real life, but it is a long-time entertainment convention. CLAMP was having a little crabby fun with the names of the attacks in this sequence.

KANI-NABE SENKAI!*

Kuro-tan

I THINK IF YOU TRY TO GET INVOLVED, HE'LL GET REALLY MAD.

KURO-TAN'S LIKE THAT.

The pet names that Fai always chooses for Kurogane aren't actually honorifics. Although they are similar in meaning to -chan, they are usually invented by young women who want to appear cute and add cute sounds to the names of people in their inner circle (close female friends and boyfriends). These syllables make the name sound almost babylike, and so Fai giving those names to gruff Kurogane is massively inappropriate, and as such, very funny.

Drawbacks to Hanshin's People

Sorata's list of complaints about the people of the Hanshin Republic are common conceptions that Tokyoites have for the people of Osaka. Their stand-up comedy is famous for a Laurel and Hardy dynamic where one person says something dumb, and the other hits him over the head for it. And yes, they do throw themselves into the dirty, polluted river when the Hanshin Tigers win the national championship.

THEY HATE LOSING; THEY NEVER GET TO THE POINT; THEY'LL ATTACK IF YOU'RE NOT PAYING ATTENTION; IF OUR TEAM WINS THEY GO CRAZY; THEY THROW THEMSELVES IN THE RIVER . . .

Kurogane's Language

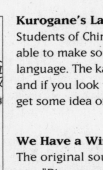

Students of Chinese or Japanese may be able to make some sense out of Kurogane's language. The kanji in his word balloons are real, and if you look them up, you should be able to get some idea of what he is saying.

We Have a Winner!

The original sound effect here was "Pin-pon, pin-pon," the universal sound (in Japan) for a correct answer in a quiz show.

> WHO IS THE ONE WHO WROTE THIS LETTER?!

Primela's Legion of Fans
Yes, CLAMP's depiction of Primela's fans is an exaggeration, but not by all that much...

"Is Everyone Having Fun?"
The Japanese phrase here is actually "Minna genki?" Similar to "Hello, Cleveland!" this is a standard phrase for a singer to say as a concert is beginning.

> A TUDOR WHO TOOTED A *FRUIT* TRIED TO TUTOR TWO *DOODOOS* TO TOOT!

Tongue Twister 1
Like English, Japanese has a large variety of tongue twisters, and here some of the more famous are misquoted by Primela. "Tonari no Kyaku wa yoku kaki kuu kyaku da" ("The guest next door eats a lot of persimmon"). But Primela said, "Tonari no gaki wa yoku kyaku kuu gaki da" ("The brat next door eats a lot of guests").

THE SIXTH SHEIK'S *SICKO'S SHIP'S SUNK!*

Tongue Twister 2

The tongue twister Primela wanted to say was, "Nama-mugi, nama-gome, nama-tamago" ("Raw barley, raw rice, raw egg"), but she got one word wrong. "Nama-gome" became "Nama-gomi" ("Raw garbage").

Tongue Twister 3

Primela tried to say, "Aka maki-gami, ao maki-gami, ki maki-gami" ("Red rolled paper, blue rolled paper, yellow rolled paper"), but she stumbled over the last words so it came out, "Maki-maki" ("rolled rolled").

RED LORRY, YELLOW LORRY, RED LORRY, YELLOW *YORRY!*

Tongue Twister 4

Primela was out of tongue twisters at this point, and she just started stringing words together like "pond skater," "red," and "aeiou."

A FLEA AND A FLY FLEW UP IN A FLUE, EE-AI-EE-AI-OH!

"Call me idiot!"

The word for fool, "baka," that many fans know already, is Tokyo dialect. A different word for fool, "aho," is Osaka dialect. Oddly, "aho" is not terribly insulting in Osaka, but "baka" is, and the opposite is true in Tokyo. In the Japanese version, Primela called Shôgo "baka," and Shôgo replied, "At least say, 'Aho'!" He was noting that Primela was getting away from her Hanshin roots by using the word "baka."

DON'T SAY "RETARD"! CALL ME A "FOOL" OR AN "IDIOT" IF YOU LIKE.

SHÔGO-KUN, ALL YOU CARE ABOUT ARE YOUR KUDAN BATTLES! YOU RETARD!

Preview of

CLAMP

We are pleased to present to you a preview from Volume 3. This
volume will be available in November 2004.

xxxHOLiC
VOLUME 2
BY CLAMP

Kimihiro Watanuki thought he had signed up with a bunch of weirdos, and he was right! He became the unfortunate indentured servant of a woman known as Yûko Ichihara, who was widely rumored to be the time-space witch. Now his voyage through the worlds of the occult are off and running, as he and Yûko go visiting fortune tellers and horoscope readers. But can the future really be told?

Meanwhile, the romance is heating up between Kimihiro and cute Himawari-chan. Then fate throws Kimihiro's old rival back into his life. Now Yûko invites all three to a temple to tell scary stories throughout the night. Is it just for fun or is there some deeper reason?

VOLUME 2: On sale July 2004 • VOLUME 3: On sale October 2004

For more information and to sign up for Del Rey's manga e-newsletter, visit www.delreymanga.com

Negima!
by Ken Akamatsu
Creator of *Love Hina!*

Ten-year-old prodigy Negi Springfield has just graduated from magic academy. He dreams of becoming a master wizard. Instead he's sent to Japan to teach English . . . at an all-girls high school! All the students are delighted with their cute new teacher—except for Asuna, who resents Negi for replacing the teacher she secretly has a crush on. Although he is forbidden to display his magical powers, sometimes Negi can't resist. And when Asuna discovers Negi's secret, she vows to make his life as difficult as possible. But no matter what, it's up to Negi to guide his class through the trials of high school life—and whatever other adventures may come their way.

TOMARE!

[STOP!]

You're going the wrong way!

Manga is a completely different type of reading experience.

To start at the *beginning*, go to the *end*!

That's right! Authentic manga is read the traditional Japanese way—from right to left. Exactly the *opposite* of how American books are read. It's easy to follow: Just go to the other end of the book, and read each page—and each panel—from right side to left side, starting at the top right. Now you're experiencing manga as it was meant to be.